This book belongs to:

....

Dedicated to all the teachers, teaching assistants and librarians
who instil and nurture a love of storytelling.

Also by Chris Naylor-Ballesteros

Tiny Reindeer

When the Storm Came

This paperback edition first published in 2024 by Andersen Press Ltd.

First published in Great Britain in 2023 by Andersen Press Ltd., 20 Vauxhall Bridge Road, London, SW1V 2SA, UK · Vijverlaan 48, 3062 HL Rotterdam, Nederland

Copyright © Chris Naylor-Ballesteros 2023. The right of Chris Naylor-Ballesteros to be identified as the author and illustrator of this work

has been asserted by him in accordance with the Copyright, Designs and Patents Act, 1988. All rights reserved. Printed and bound in China.

British Library Cataloguing in Publication Data available. ISBN 978 1 83913 274 2   10   9   8   7   6   5   4   3   2   1

BELLA
the Storyteller

Chris Naylor-Ballesteros

Andersen Press

Hello there!

I'm not the squirrel, and I'm not the rabbit either. No, I'm Bella – the **background.** I'm *everything* else in this book, the fields and trees, the flowers, the sky and clouds. Everything.

But this time, just for once, I'd like to be Bella the STORYTELLER. I'm going to tell you an *amazing* story.
Now, I just need some characters . . .

Hi Squirrel! Hi Rabbit! I'm going to tell a story!

Do you want to be in it?

So ... first, I think our story needs a huge, smouldering VOLCANO!

What do you think?

Not quite sure about that, to be honest.

Aren't huge, smouldering volcanoes a bit dangerous?

Oh come on, it's MILES away!

Then, all of a sudden there's a . . .

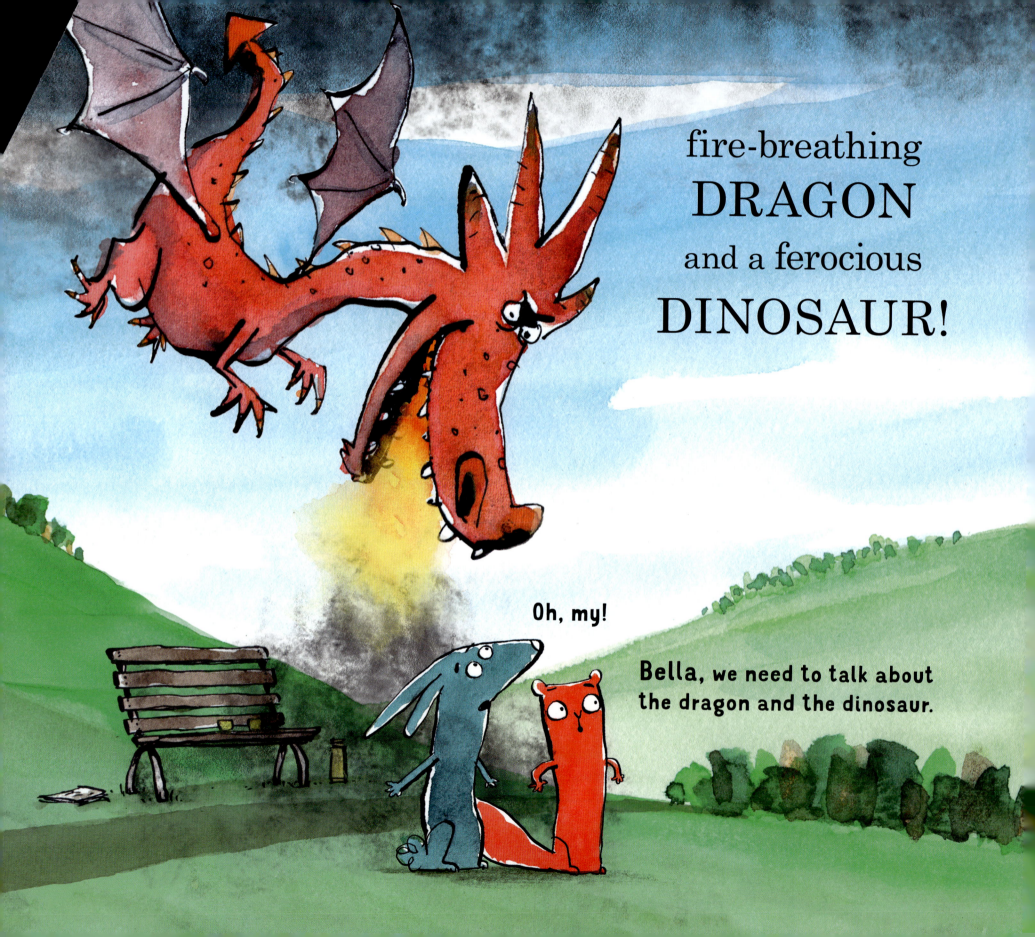

Aren't they
just brilliant?
Then we'll have . . .

No it *isn't!* And absolutely everybody
LOVES unicorns! That's a FACT.
Wait. I've just had **another great idea!**
Let's have . . .

PIRATES,
SHARKS,
a SINKING SHIP
and a SEA
MONSTER!

Let's mix *everything* together –
VOLCANO! DRAGON!
DINOSAUR! UNICORNS!
PIRATES! SHARK!
and a SEA MONSTER!

HELP!

Oh, can't you
two please just
try to enjoy
yourselves?

RIGHT. I've tried my best. But if you're determined to spoil everything and **not** have fun, then FINE.

Turn the page and it will all go away.

Just

like

that!

Rabbit – we're
saved! But where
did everything go?

I don't know,
Squirrel. Hello? Is
anybody there?
Bella? Please come
back, Bella.

Hello, Rabbit. Hello, Squirrel. It's Bella.

Okay. You didn't like my story very much, did you?

Not really, Bella. It was a bit of a jumble, wasn't it?

Maybe Squirrel and I should tell a story now – a nice, quiet bedtime story.

Oh I LOVE bedtime stories! Can I help? Pleeeease!

Just look at what I can do – a beautiful
night sky full of stars. Isn't that lovely?

Well yes, it is. But
remember, Bella – we're
going to tell a nice,
quiet, bedtime story,
OK? No sea monsters!

Or dinosaurs!
Or dragons or
sharks or
pirates or . . .

Oh, certainly not! But what if it's a bedtime story . . .

...in SPACE!

I've got a very
bad feeling
about this...

Bella! What's that zooming towards us?

Okay, spoilsports! Here you are – safe and sound.
You can tell your sleepy bedtime story now!

Also by Chris Naylor-Ballesteros

Tiny Reindeer

When the Storm Came

Find out more at www.andersenpress.co.uk